W9-BBP-882

DISCARD

CHICAGO PUBLIC LIBRARY
VODAK EASTSIDE BRANCH
3710 E. 106TH STREET
CHICAGO, IL 60617

DISCARD

Dear Parent:
Your child's love of reading starts here!

Every child learns to read in a different way and at his or her own speed. Some go back and forth between reading levels and read favorite books again and again. Others read through each level in order. You can help your young reader improve and become more confident by encouraging his or her own interests and abilities. From books your child reads with you to the first books he or she reads alone, there are I Can Read Books for every stage of reading:

SHARED READING
Basic language, word repetition, and whimsical illustrations, ideal for sharing with your emergent reader

BEGINNING READING
Short sentences, familiar words, and simple concepts for children eager to read on their own

READING WITH HELP
Engaging stories, longer sentences, and language play for developing readers

READING ALONE
Complex plots, challenging vocabulary, and high-interest topics for the independent reader

ADVANCED READING
Short paragraphs, chapters, and exciting themes for the perfect bridge to chapter books

I Can Read Books have introduced children to the joy of reading since 1957. Featuring award-winning authors and illustrators and a fabulous cast of beloved characters, I Can Read Books set the standard for beginning readers.

A lifetime of discovery begins with the magical words **"I Can Read!"**

Visit www.icanread.com for information
on enriching your child's reading experience.

I Can Read!

BEGINNING
1
READING

Ruby's
Perfect Day

by Susan Hill
pictures by Margie Moore

HarperCollins*Publishers*

HarperCollins®, ♣®, and I Can Read Book® are trademarks of HarperCollins Publishers Inc.

Ruby's Perfect Day Text copyright © 2006 by Susan Hill Illustrations copyright © 2006 by Margie Moore All rights reserved. No part of this book may be used or reproduced in any manner whatsoever without written permission except in the case of brief quotations embodied in critical articles and reviews. Printed in the United States of America. For information address HarperCollins Children's Books, a division of HarperCollins Publishers, 1350 Avenue of the Americas, New York, NY 10019. www.harperchildrens.com

Library of Congress Cataloging-in-Publication Data
Hill, Susan.
  Ruby's perfect day / by Susan Hill ; pictures by Margie Moore.
      p. cm. — (An I can read book)
  Summary: When Ruby Raccoon wants to share a perfectly sunny day with her busy woodland friends, she discovers that perfect days can be spent all by yourself.
  ISBN-10: 0-06-008982-2 (trade bdg.) — ISBN-10: 0-06-008983-0 (lib. bdg.)
  ISBN-13: 978-0-06-008982-5 (trade bdg.) — ISBN-13: 978-0-06-008983-2 (lib. bdg.)
  [1. Solitude—Fiction. 2. Day—Fiction. 3. Friendship—Fiction.] I. Moore, Margie, ill. II. Title. III. Series.
PZ7.H5574Rum 2006   2005014516
[E]—dc22

1   2   3   4   5   6   7   8   9   10   ❖   First Edition

R0411781697

For Sara
—S.H.

For Jerry
—M.M.

Ruby Raccoon woke up and stretched.

The sun was shining.

The birds were singing.

The air smelled fresh and sweet.

"This is a perfect day," said Ruby.

Ruby's tummy rumbled.

"It's a perfect day

for a big breakfast!"

Ruby knocked

at the door of Fiona Fox.

"Fiona," said Ruby,

"will you have breakfast with me?"

"I'm sorry, Ruby," said Fiona.

"I'm too busy to have breakfast
with you today."

"That's okay," said Ruby.

11

Ruby walked home and
made a big breakfast.

She ate enough for two
and got a little tummy ache.

13

After breakfast,

Ruby sat at her table

under the big tree.

"This is a perfect day," said Ruby.

The sun made a pattern on the table.

"A perfect day

for a game of checkers!"

Just then Dan Duck waddled by.

"Dan," called Ruby,

"will you play checkers with me?"

"I'm sorry, Ruby," said Dan.

"I'm too busy to play checkers."

"That's okay," said Ruby.

Ruby sat at her table and
made a checkerboard of leaves.
It was a pretty checkerboard,
but the wind blew it away.

19

The sun moved higher in the sky.

Ruby walked to the top of the hill.

"This is a perfect day," said Ruby.

An acorn fell to the ground

and rolled a few feet.

"A perfect day

for a roll down the hill!"

Ruby saw Bunny Rabbit hopping by.

"Bunny!" shouted Ruby.

"Will you roll down the hill with me?"

"Sorry! Too busy!" Bunny cried.

"Okay," called Ruby.

Ruby rolled down the hill

and landed with a bump

at the bottom.

Then she walked home

and sat on a stump

in the afternoon sun.

Ruby thought about her day.

She had made a big breakfast.

She had played

a new kind of checkers.

And she had rolled

down the hill—fast!

"This is a perfect day," said Ruby.

Ruby saw a worm wiggling in the mud.

"A perfect day

to work in my garden!"

Ruby began to dig.

She dug and she dug.

She hummed as she dug.

"This is a perfect day," said Ruby.

"A perfect day

for being all by myself!"